This Little Tiger book belongs to:

_____

_____

_____

For Toad, the dog with
the itchy back
~D.B.

For Bentley, our very
own shaggy dog
~G.W.

This edition produced 2006 for
BOOKS ARE FUN LTD
1680 Hwy 1 North, Fairfield, Iowa, IA 52556
by LITTLE TIGER PRESS
An imprint of Magi Publications
1 The Coda Centre, 189 Munster Road, London SW6 6AW
www.littletigerpress.com
First published in Great Britain 2001
by Little Tiger Press, London
Text copyright © David Bedford 2001
Illustrations copyright © Gwyneth Williamson 2001
Printed in China
1 3 5 7 9 10 8 6 4 2

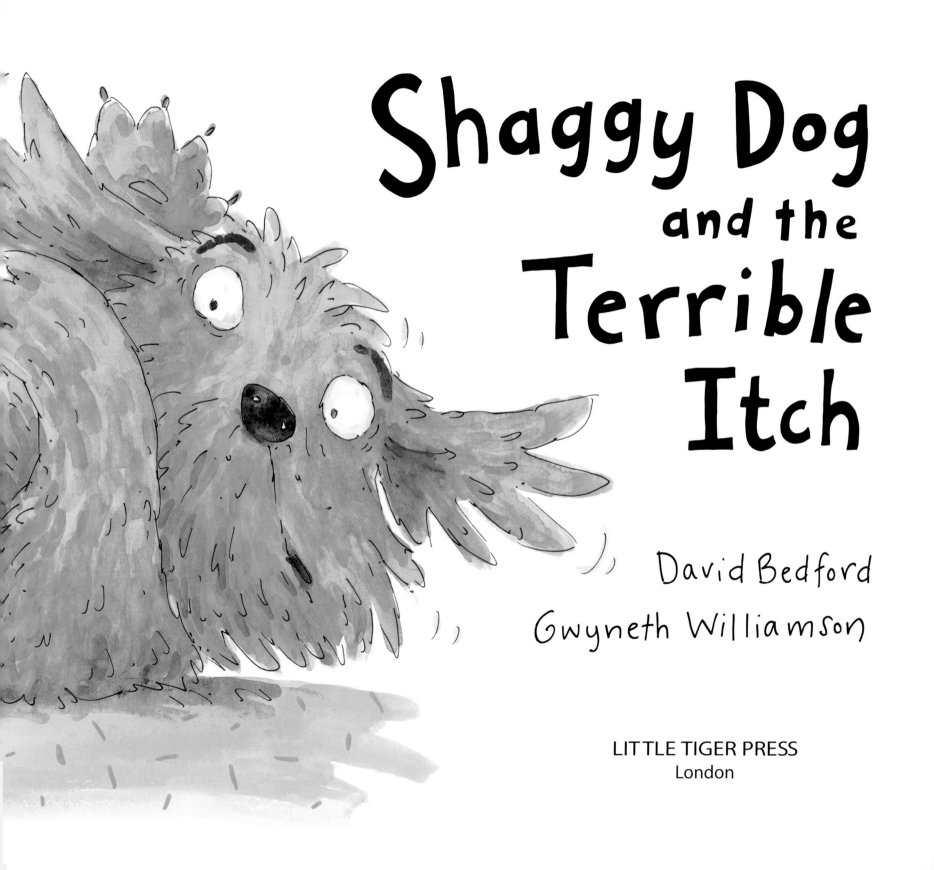

Shaggy Dog
and the
Terrible
Itch

David Bedford

Gwyneth Williamson

LITTLE TIGER PRESS
London

Shaggy Dog had an itch on his back.
He scratched against a tree but . . .

his back was still itchy.

"Will you scratch my back?"
Shaggy Dog asked Mimi the poodle.
"Ugh!" said Mimi, "scratch your
back, *no thank you!* I'm off to
the Poodle Parlor for a
wash and trim."

"*I* will scratch your back," said Farmer Gertie. "But first you must help me round up my sheep."

The sheep were hiding, and it took
ages to find them.
"*Woof woof!*" barked Shaggy Dog.
"Come here, sheep, come here *now*!"

At last the sheep were locked in their pen.
Farmer Gertie used her curly crook to scratch
Shaggy Dog's back.
"Ooh!" said Shaggy Dog. "That's much better."
But as Shaggy Dog walked into town . . .

Shaggy Dog knocked on
the window of Merv's Café.

*the itch
came back!*

"Who will scratch the Itch from my back?" he asked.
"*I* will," said Merv. "But first you must
wash my pots and pans."

Shaggy Dog washed towers and towers of pots and pans. Bubbles covered his legs and got into his mouth, and when he had finished, his paws were all wrinkly.

Merv used a long fork to
scratch Shaggy Dog's back.
"Ooh, ooh!" said Shaggy Dog.
"That's much, much better."
But when Shaggy Dog left
the café . . .

the itch came back!

Shaggy Dog popped into
Mary Lou's Poodle Parlor.

"Will you scratch the Itch from my back?"
asked Shaggy Dog.
"Okay," said Mary Lou. "But only if you
brush up the fur on the floor."

Shaggy Dog brushed up
mountains and mountains
of poodle fur.

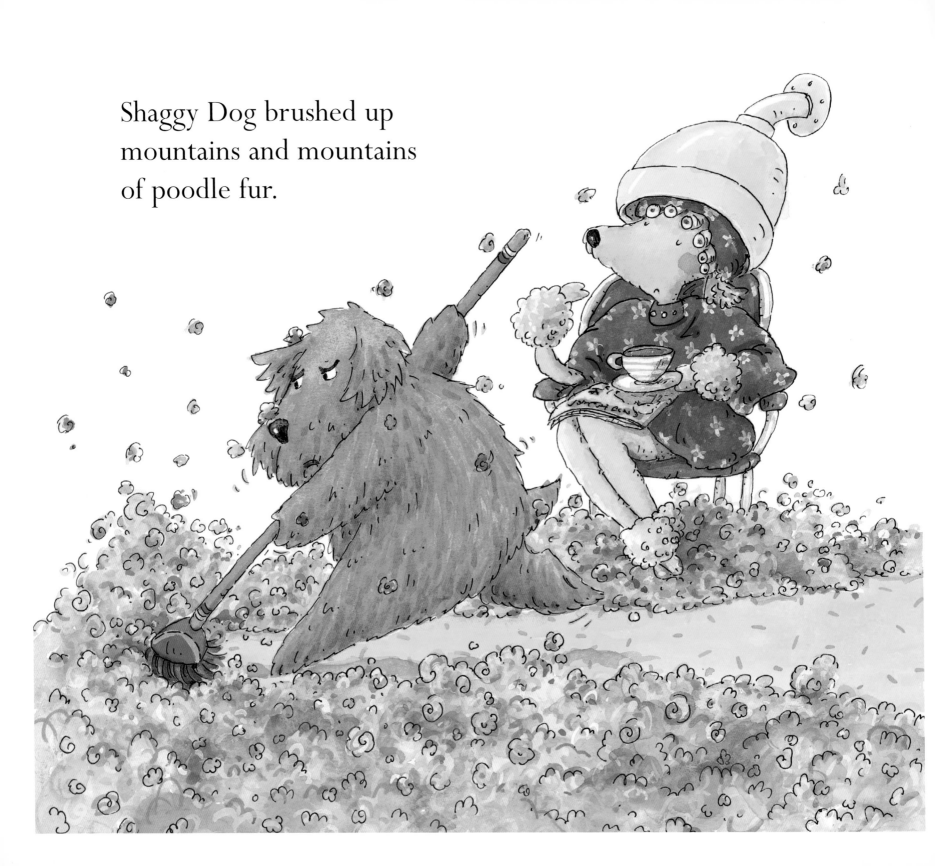

Fur got up his nose, and when he had finished, he had fur in his ears and his eyes, too.

Aitchoo!
Aitchoo!
Aitchoo!

he sneezed.

Shaggy Dog shook out all the fur, and Mary Lou used the poodle brush to scratch his back.

"Ooh, ooh, ooh!" said Shaggy Dog. "That's much, much, MUCH better." But when Mary Lou stopped scratching . . .

the itch came back!

"What can I do?" asked
Shaggy Dog.
"Sit in the chair," said
Mary Lou. "I'll wash
and trim you."

The bubbly shampoo soothed
Shaggy Dog's back.
"Ooh, ooh, ooh, OOOH!" said
Shaggy Dog.

The poodle scissors tickled and went

Snip! Snip! Snip!

"Hee, hee, hee," giggled Shaggy Dog.

When Mary Lou had finished trimming Shaggy Dog's fur . . .

Shaggy Dog felt

Wonderful!!

The Itch had gone at last . . .

but where did it go?